This book belongs to

MOTHER GOOSE

THE CHILDREN'S CLASSIC EDITION

MOTHER GOOSE

THE CHILDREN'S CLASSIC EDITION

with illustrations by

LEON BAXTER · GRAHAM PERCY · GARY REES

KAY WIDDOWSON · JENNY WILLIAMS

Colour
Library
Direct

CLD 20666
This edition published in 1998 for Colour Library Direct,
Godalming Business Centre, Woolsack Way,
Godalming, Surrey GU7 1XW
Printed in China

9 8 7 6 5 4 3 2 1
Digit on the right indicates the number of this printing.

Cover and interior design by Ian Butterworth

Cover illustration by Graham Percy
Interior illustrations by Leon Baxter, Gary Rees,
Kay Widdowson, and Jenny Williams

Edited by Tara Ann McFadden

Text set in Goudy

Published by Courage Books, an imprint of
Running Press Book Publishers
125 South Twenty-second Street
Philadelphia, Pennsylvania 19103-4399

INTRODUCTION

Mother Goose is both a character in and a teller of the best-known rhymes in the world. This volume contains many of the greatest rhymes for children of all ages. The rhymes represent a heritage that has been passed down for generations since eighteenth-century Europe. This tradition of story telling, ballads, and folk songs began as a form of adult entertainment. The rhymes were originally recited by parents, but children became attracted to their rhythm and witty verse and took the rhymes as their own.

Children continue to love these rhymes. They are exposed to them as little babies in the form of everyone's favorite lullaby, "Rock-a-Bye Baby," and in their first clapping game, "Pat-a-Cake." What child doesn't love to have her toes tickled during "This Little Piggy"?

The characters in these rhymes are already old friends to your child. With the help of Little Miss Muffet, Humpty Dumpty, Jack and Jill, Little Bo-Peep, and many more, children will love the wonderful tradition of rhyming verse and parents will be able to revisit the characters that were so prominent in their own youth.

This volume includes bright, happy, silly, and never-before-seen illustrations by some of the most talented artists of our time. Open these pages and visit a wonderfully magical world where eggs can talk and cats play fiddles. Share with your child the magical world of Mother Goose.

CONTENTS

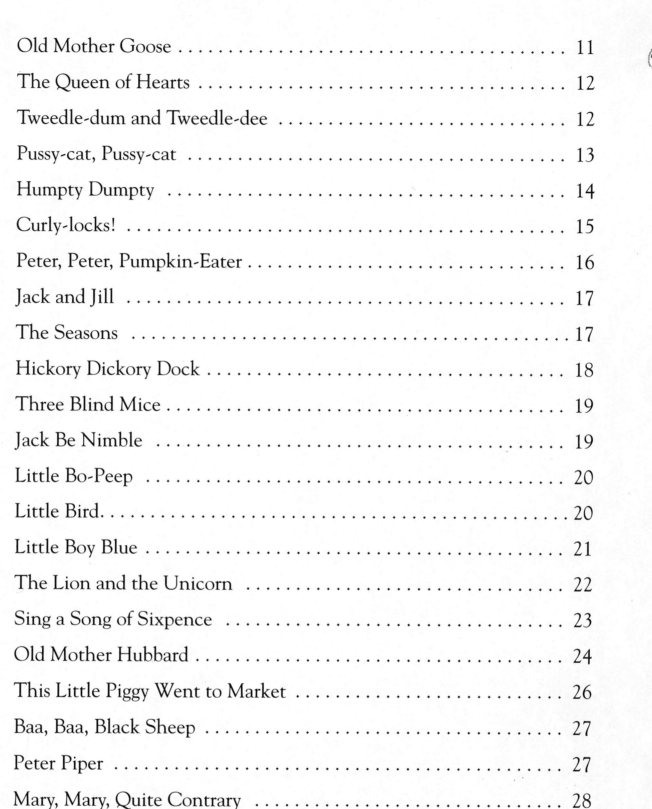
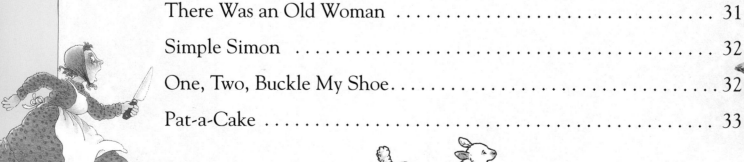

CONTENTS

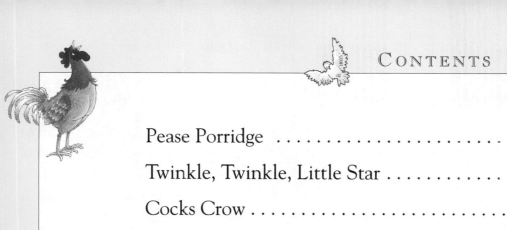

Old Mother Goose, when
She wanted to wander,
Would ride through the air
On a very fine gander.

The Queen of Hearts,
She made some tarts,
All on a summer's day;
The Knave of Hearts,
He stole the tarts,
And took them clean away.

The King of Hearts
Called for the tarts,
And beat the Knave full sore.
The Knave of Hearts
Brought back the tarts,
And vowed he'd steal no more.

Tweedle-dum and Tweedle-dee
Resolved to have a battle,
For Tweedle-dum said Tweedle-dee
Had spoiled his nice, new rattle.
Just then flew by a monstrous crow,
As big as a tarbarrel,
Which frightened both the heroes so,
They quite forgot their quarrel.

"Pussy-cat, pussy-cat, where have you been?"
"I've been to London to look at the Queen."
"Pussy-cat, pussy-cat, what did you there?"
"I frightened a little mouse under the chair."

Humpty Dumpty sat on a wall,
Humpty Dumpty had a great fall;

All the king's horses, and all the king's men
Couldn't put Humpty Dumpty together again.

Curly-locks, Curly-locks, wilt thou be mine?
Thou shalt not wash dishes, nor yet feed the swine;
But sit on a cushion, and sew a fine seam,
And feed upon strawberries, sugar, and cream!

Peter, Peter, pumpkin-eater,
Had a wife and couldn't keep her;
He put her in a pumpkin shell,
And there he kept her very well.

Peter, Peter, pumpkin-eater,
Had another, and didn't love her.
Peter learned to read and spell,
And then he loved her very well.

Jack and Jill went up the hill,
To fetch a pail of water;
Jack fell down, and broke his crown,
And Jill came tumbling after.

Spring is showery, flowery, bowery;
Summer: hoppy, croppy, poppy;
Autumn: wheezy, sneezy, freezy;
Winter: slippy, drippy, nippy.

Hickory,
     dickory,
          dock!

The mouse ran up the clock;

The
  clock
     struck
        one,

And down he run,

Hickory,
     dickory,
          dock!

Three blind mice! See how they run!
They all ran after the farmer's wife,
Who cut off their tails with a carving knife.
Did you ever see such a sight in your life
As three blind mice?

Jack be nimble,
Jack be quick,
Jack jump over the candlestick.

Little Bo-Peep has lost her sheep,
And can't tell where to find them;
Leave them alone, and they'll come home,
And bring their tails behind them.

Once I saw a little bird come
hop, hop, hop;
So I cried, "Little bird,
Will you stop, stop, stop?"

And was going to the window
To say, "How do you do?"
But he shook his little tail,
And far away he flew.

Little Boy Blue, come, blow your horn!
The sheep's in the meadow, the cow's in the corn.
Where's the little boy that looks after the sheep?
Under the haystack, fast asleep!

The Lion and the Unicorn were fighting for the crown,
The Lion beat the Unicorn all around the town.

Some gave them white bread, and some gave them brown,
Some gave them plum-cake, and sent them out of town.

Sing a song of sixpence,
A pocket full of rye,
Four-and-twenty blackbirds
Baked in a pie!

When the pie was opened
The birds began to sing:
Was not that a dainty dish
To set before the king?

The king was in his counting-house,
Counting out his money;
The queen was in the parlor,
Eating bread and honey.

The maid was in the garden,
Hanging out the clothes;
When down came a blackbird
And snapped off her nose.

Old Mother Hubbard
Went to the cupboard,
To give her poor dog a bone;
But when she got there
The cupboard was bare,
And so the poor dog had none.

She went to the baker's
To buy him some bread,
When she came back
The poor dog was dead.

She went to the undertaker's
To buy him a coffin;
When she came back
The poor dog was laughing.

She took a clean dish
To get him some tripe;
When she came back
He was smoking a pipe.

She went to the alehouse
To get him some beer;
When she came back
The dog sat in a chair.

She went to the tavern
For white wine and red;
When she came back
The dog stood on his head.

She went to the hatter's
To buy him a hat;
When she came back
He was feeding the cat.

She went to the fruiterer's
To buy him some fruit;
When she came back
He was playing the flute.

She went to the cobbler's
To buy him some shoes;
When she came back
He was reading the news.

She went to the hosier's
To buy him some hose;
When she came back
He was dressed in his clothes.

She went to the barber's
To buy him a wig;
When she came back
He was dancing a jig.

She went to the tailor's
To buy him a coat;
When she came back
He was riding a goat.

She went to the seamstress's
To buy him some linen;
When she came back
The dog was a-spinning.

The dame made a curtsey,
The dog made a bow;
The dame said, "Your servant,"
The dog said, "Bow-wow."

This little piggy went to market;

This little piggy stayed at home;

This little piggy had roast beef;

This little piggy had none;

This little piggy went, "Wee, wee, wee" all the way home.

Baa, baa, black sheep,
Have you any wool?
Yes sir, yes sir,
Three bags full;
One for my master,
One for my dame,
And one for the little boy
Who lives down the lane.

Peter Piper picked a peck
of pickled peppers;
A peck of pickled peppers
Peter Piper picked.
If Peter Piper picked
a peck of pickled peppers,
Where's the peck of pickled peppers
Peter Piper picked?

Mary, Mary, quite contrary,
How does your garden grow?
Silver bells, and cockle-shells,
And pretty maids all in a row.

Little Miss Muffet
Sat on a tuffet,
Eating her curds and whey;
Along came a spider,
Who sat down beside her,
And frightened Miss Muffet away.

There was a crooked man,
And he went a crooked mile,
He found a crooked sixpence
Beside a crooked stile;
He bought a crooked cat,
Which caught a crooked mouse,
And they all lived together
In a little crooked house.

There was an old woman
Who lived in a shoe.
She had so many children
She didn't know what to do.
She gave them some broth
Without any bread.
She whipped them all soundly
And put them to bed.

Simple Simon met a pieman,
Going to the fair;
Says Simple Simon to the pieman,
"Let me taste your ware."

Says the pieman to Simple Simon,
"Show me first your penny".
Says Simple Simon to the pieman,
"Indeed, I have not any."

One, two, buckle my shoe;
Three, four, knock at the door;
Five, six, pick up sticks;
Seven, eight, lay them straight;
Nine, ten, a good fat hen;
Eleven, twelve, dig and delve;
Thirteen, fourteen, maids a-courting;
Fifteen, sixteen, maids in the kitchen;
Seventeen, eighteen, maids a-waiting;
Nineteen, twenty, my plate's empty.

Pat-a-cake, pat-a-cake, baker's man,
Bake me a cake as fast as you can.
Pat it and prick it,
And mark it with a T,
Put it in the oven for Tommy and me.

Pease porridge hot,
Pease porridge cold,
Pease porridge in the pot,
Nine days old.

Some like it hot,
Some like it cold,
Some like it in the pot,
Nine days old.

Twinkle, twinkle, little star,
How I wonder what you are!
Up above the world so high,
Like a diamond in the sky.

Cocks crow in the morn to tell us to rise,
And he who lies late will never be wise;
For early to bed and early to rise,
Is the way to be healthy and wealthy and wise.

Wee Willie Winkie
Runs through the town,
Upstairs and downstairs,
In his night gown;
Rapping at the window,
Crying through the lock,
"Are the children in their beds?
Now it's eight o'clock."

Here we go round the mulberry bush,
The mulberry bush, the mulberry bush.
Here we go round the mulberry bush,
On a cold and frosty morning.

The little robin grieves
When the snow is on the ground,
For the trees have no leaves,
And no berries can be found.

The air is cold, the worms are hid;
For robin here what can be done?
Let's throw around some crumbs of bread,
And then he'll eat till snow is gone.

To market, to market, to buy a fat pig,
Home again, home again, jiggety jig.
To market, to market, to buy a plum bun,
Home again, home again, market is done.

Girls and boys,
    come out to play,
The moon doth shine
    as bright as day;
Leave your supper,
    and leave your sleep,
And come with your playfellows
    into the street.
Come with a whoop,
    come with a call,
Come with a good
    will or not at all.

Hush-a-bye baby
on the tree top,
When the wind blows
the cradle will rock;
When the bough breaks
the cradle will fall;
Down will come baby,
bough, cradle and all.

So vast is the prowess of Harry the Great,
He'll pluck a hair from the pale-faced moon;
Or a lion familiarly take by the tooth,
And lead him about as you lead a baboon.

As I was going to St. Ives
I met a man with seven wives.
Every wife had seven sacks,
Every sack had seven cats,
Every cat had seven kits.
Kits, cats, sacks, and wives,
How many were going to St. Ives?

Hey, diddle, diddle!
The cat and the fiddle,
The cow jumped over the moon;
The little dog laughed
To see such sport,
And the dish ran away
with the spoon.

This is the house that Jack built.
This is the malt
That lay in the house that Jack built.

This is the rat,
That ate the malt
That lay in the house that Jack built.

This is the cat,
That killed the rat,
That ate the malt
That lay in the house that Jack built.

This is the dog,
That worried the cat,
That killed the rat,
That ate the malt
That lay in the house that Jack built.

This is the cow with the crumpled horn,
That tossed the dog,
That worried the cat,
That killed the rat,
That ate the malt
That lay in the house that Jack built.

Turn the page

This is the maiden all forlorn,
That milked the cow with the crumpled horn,
That tossed the dog,
That worried the cat,
That killed the rat,
That ate the malt
That lay in the house that Jack built.

This is the man all tattered and torn,
That kissed the maiden all forlorn,
That milked the cow with the crumpled horn,
That tossed the dog,
That worried the cat,
That killed the rat,
That ate the malt
That lay in the house that Jack built.

This is the priest all shaven and shorn,
That married the man all tattered and torn,
That kissed the maiden all forlorn,
That milked the cow with the crumpled horn,
That tossed the dog,
That worried the cat,
That killed the rat,
That ate the malt
That lay in the house that Jack built.

This is the cock that crowed in the morn,
That waked the priest all shaven and shorn,
That married the man all tattered and torn,
That kissed the maiden all forlorn,
That milked the cow with the crumpled horn,
That tossed the dog,
That worried the cat,
That killed the rat,
That ate the malt
That lay in the house that Jack built.

This is the farmer sowing the corn,
That kept the cock that crowed in the morn,
That waked the priest all shaven and shorn,
That married the man all tattered and torn,
That kissed the maiden all forlorn,
That milked the cow with the crumpled horn,
That tossed the dog,
That worried the cat,
That killed the rat,
That ate the malt
That lay in the house that Jack built.

I saw a ship a-sailing,
A-sailing on the sea;
And, oh! it was all laden
With pretty things for thee!

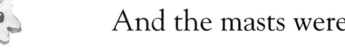

There were comfits in the cabin,
And apples in the hold;
The sails were made of silk,
And the masts were made of gold.

The four-and-twenty sailors
That stood between the decks,
Were four-and-twenty white mice
With chains about their necks.

The captain was a duck,
With a packet on his back;
And when the ship began to move,
The captain said, "Quack! Quack!"

Rub-a-dub-dub,
Three men in a tub,
And who do you think they be?
The butcher, the baker,
And candlestick-maker,
Turn 'em out,
Knaves all three!

Jack Sprat
Could eat no fat,
His wife could eat no lean;
And so,
Betwixt them both
They licked the platter clean.

At the siege of Belleisle
I was there all the while,
All the while, all the while,
At the siege of Belleisle.

This is the way the gentlemen ride,
Gallop-a-trot,
Gallop-a-trot!
This is the way the gentlemen ride,
Gallop-a-gallop-a-trot!

Ride a cock-horse to Banbury Cross,
To see a fine lady upon a white horse.
Rings on her fingers, and bells on her toes,
She shall have music wherever she goes.

Molly, my sister, and I fell out,
And what do you think it was all about?
She loved coffee and I loved tea,
And that was the reason we couldn't agree.

The King of France went up the hill,
With twenty thousand men;
The King of France came down the hill,
And ne'er went up again.

What are little boys made of?
What are little boys made of?
"Snaps and snails, and puppy-dogs' tails;
And that's what little boys are made of."

Little Jack Horner
Sat in the corner,
Eating of Christmas pie:
He put in his thumb,
And pulled out a plum,
And said, "What a good boy am I!"

Hector Protector was dressed all in green;
Hector Protector was sent to the Queen.
The Queen did not like him,
No more did the King;
So Hector Protector was sent back again.

Tom, Tom, the piper's son,
Stole a pig, and away he run.
The pig was eat,
And Tom was beat,
And Tom ran crying down the street.

Mary had a little lamb,
Its fleece was white as snow;
And everywhere that Mary went
The lamb was sure to go.

It followed her to school one day,
Which was against the rule;
It made the children laugh and play,
To see a lamb in school.

Old King Cole
Was a merry old soul,
And a merry old soul was he;
He called for his pipe,
And he called for his bowl,
And he called for his fiddlers three!

I won't be my father's Jack,
I won't be my father's Jill;
I will be the fiddler's wife,
And have music when I will.

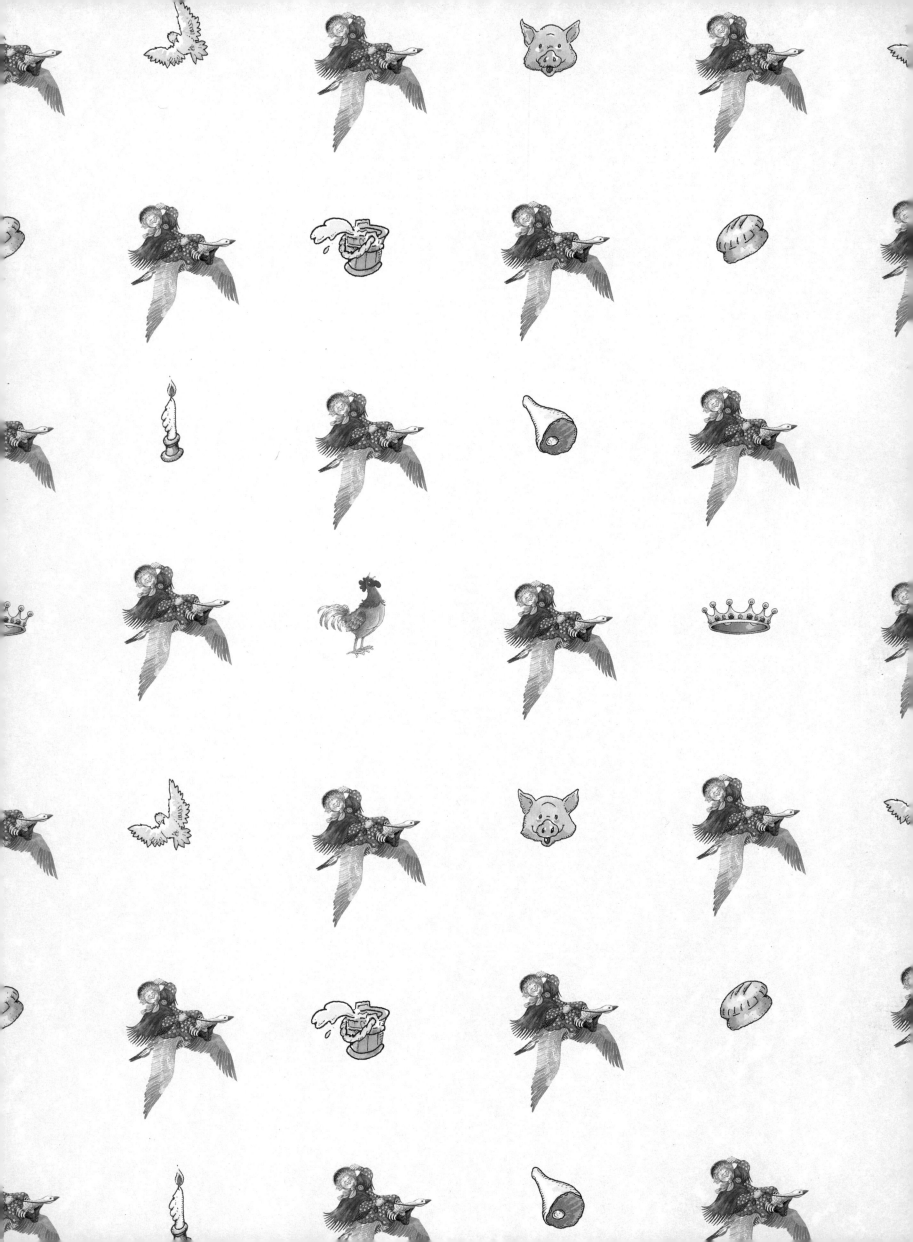